Ghost stories

Mary Chapman
Gillian Philip
Anne Rooney
John Townsend

Ransom

SHADES 2.0 SHORTS

Ghost Stories

by Gillian Philip, Mary Chapman, Anne Rooney and John Townsend

Published by Ransom Publishing Ltd.

Radley House, 8 St. Cross Road, Winchester, Hampshire SO23 9HX, UK

www.ransom.co.uk

ISBN   978 178127 223 7

Misty and The Hanging Tree first published in 2009

This edition published by Ransom Publishing 2013

CONTENTS

Misty

by Gillian Philip

Misty

by Gillian Philip

'Now who – ?' Thea did a double take and
braked.

The man on the bypass wasn't your
average hitchhiker. He was sharply dressed,
in a well-cut suit and a blue-green silk tie.

Oh. Thea blinked. Of course: how had
she forgotten that pile-up back there? Now
she remembered the glimpse of crushed

metal beyond the ambulances. How had this guy climbed out of that wreckage and staggered away? Maybe he'd been thrown clear. A head injury? He probably didn't know where he was. A bit lax of the paramedics.

Shaking her head, Thea glanced at her watch: only half-eight. She pulled over and shoved open the passenger door.

'Can I take you to the hospital?'

Bending down, the man peered in at Thea. There was something familiar about him, but Thea couldn't place it. She couldn't place much this morning, with this headache. God, she felt awful. Vague and hungover. Should have called in sick.

He rubbed his forehead, smearing blood, then frowned as he looked at his fingers.

'That's good of you. You sure it's no trouble, er – ?'

'Thea. Thea Madeley. Here, get in. You look terrible.'

'I'm sure I do.'

The man sank gratefully into the passenger seat and tugged the door shut. When he turned to Thea, though, he wore an unexpected grin.

'D'you know, I just knew it was you. Soon as I saw your face through the car window, I thought: that's young Thea. One of my favourite pupils! Can't believe you're old enough to drive.'

'Passed my test a month ago.' Thea frowned. 'Sorry, but I – '

'Don't remember me? Well, you'd just started Year Eight when I left teaching. Must be – four years ago? Five?'

Thea blushed. God, what was wrong with her head this morning?

'Mr Munro! Media Studies! I'm sorry, I – '

'*Harry*, seeing as you've left school. Haven't you?'

'Only this year. I've got a job on the *Eastwick Chronicle*. Just in the office, getting experience. I'm driving there now.'

'Oh. I hope this isn't an inconvenience.'

'No. It's only half-eight.' Thea pulled out her phone and checked it. No messages. 'I can text if I'm going to be late. This is an emergency.'

'Watch the road, Thea,' said Harry, giving her a wry look.

'Oh, yeah. That was quite a smash back there. How'd it happen?'

'Don't know ... ' Harry frowned.

'Maybe I should call ahead to the hospital. We'll be there in ten minutes, but – ' She peered at her phone again. 'No signal. Typical.' She prodded a button.

'Thea!' Harry tensed. 'Not while you're driving.'

'Relax.' She was completely in control, of course; Harry Munro was just on edge, and no wonder. 'I'm fine.'

'Good, good.' Harry still seemed nervous. 'Careful, Thea. There's mist in the valley ahead.'

'Oh, yes! That's where you'd expect a crash, not on the bypass. I mean, how do people manage to – sorry.' She blushed again. 'Sorry. Accidents happen, I guess.'

'I suppose.' Harry shrugged, then smiled. 'So how's the job, Thea?'

'Good! I mean, OK. It's a start.' She reddened.

It seemed less impressive, now that she'd remembered why Harry Munro left teaching. He'd gone to work for that young politician, the one who'd got everyone so excited a few years back. Passionate, sincere, charismatic: Britain's own JFK.

Matt Cornwell had come from their town – in other words, from out of nowhere. Thea remembered her dad going on about Cornwell, the way his voice filled with respect and his eyes shone. She remembered her mum actually crying about him.

She remembered it better than she remembered her own name this morning. Fizzy water and orange juice tonight. Definitely.

'I saw you on TV once. A few years back. With that Matt Cornwell.'

'Just the once?' Harry teased.

'Well, I was young. Wasn't into politics.'

Harry gave a long, sad sigh.

'You're still young, Thea.'

Harry Munro had gone with Cornwell as his press officer, fixer, minder. He'd given him a stratospheric profile; run a dynamic campaign on the internet; terrified journalists and charmed them all at once. Together, Matt Cornwell and Harry Munro had been heading for Number 10 ...

'Rotten that he died,' said Thea.

Her companion sighed again, as if the memory was still painful. Harry had given up everything for Matt Cornwell, hitching his wagon to a shining, shooting star. And then the star had fallen. Extinguished for good.

'When I think I could have been running the country by now.'

'Behind the scenes, of course,' said Thea.

'Best way to do it,' laughed Harry.

Poor guy. The end of Matt Cornwell must have been the end of Harry's glittering future, too, because Thea was sure she hadn't heard of him since. Harry had the pallor of a man with a permanent, boring desk job. Mind you, if she could get her head together, she could interview him. Hey, a scoop!

'A plane crash, of all things,' mused Harry. 'It's almost a cliché.' He shook his head in melancholy wonder.

Not long now and they'd be at the hospital. Surely the Chronicle wouldn't mind her being late if she was finding a story? Thea glanced at her watch. Half-past eight. But maybe she should check with the editor. Let him know. She checked her phone again. Still no signal.

'I wish you wouldn't do that,' said Harry.

'Don't worry,' said Thea, irritated. She added pointedly, 'Did a phone cause that crash?'

'I – ' Harry frowned. 'You know, I think it might have done.'

'Well, it's not going to happen now.'

'No. Fair enough. Silly of me.'

Harry laughed, a genuine laugh that made Thea feel quite relieved.

'Ah, well. I'm not surprised you didn't remember me at first, Thea. Nobody ever does, not after Matt. Careful, now! We're getting pretty close to that mist. Oh, I'm doing it *again*!'

Thea shot him an understanding look. Of course he was a bundle of nerves. To humour him, Thea eased off the accelerator; but despite the mist lying in the valley, the road conditions were good up here and the air was clear. There weren't even many other cars on the road.

None, in fact. That was unusual, but she'd been the last to get through before the police blocked the road and set up a diversion. Well, she must have been. She assumed she was ...

Thea punched the radio controls in search of a traffic report, but a hissing, white noise was all she could get. Wincing, she switched it off.

In the silence, she heard Harry humming cheerfully. For a guy in shock, he seemed remarkably cool. Pale, but cool.

'I am glad I met up with you.' Harry gave her a smile. 'I was supposed to, you see. After the car crash and all. One of my old pupils!'

'Fate, you reckon?' said Thea lightly.

'You could say that,' agreed Harry. 'Fate.'

Thea eyed him nervously.

'You've got to meet it some time,' added Harry. 'However young.'

Thea swallowed hard. 'What a mess it was back there.' She didn't know why her voice was trembling, or why her spine was so cold. 'You're lucky you got out of it at all.'

'I didn't, Thea.'

Into the silence leaked a low, white noise. *I thought I switched that off*, thought Thea. She punched the radio switch again, then again, harder. Harder. Frantically.

'Careful, Thea! Watch the road! *Honestly!*'

'What d'you – the crash.' Panic filled her. 'What d'you mean, *you didn't get out of it?*'

'Oh!' Harry chuckled. 'I didn't mean – oh, Lord, I'm sorry I scared you. I mean, I wasn't *involved* in the crash. You assumed that, of course. Sorry. No, no. That crash was nothing to do with me.'

Thea gave a high laugh, dizzy with relief. She felt silly and childish for even thinking it.

'Sorry. Being stupid. Imagination

running away with me.'

'Oh, Thea. That's perfectly understandable. The circumstances are a little odd, aren't they? But no, no. I didn't get out of the crash.'

Thea's reply stuck in her throat. She wanted to ask where Harry had come from, then. Why he'd been there on the roadside. Why, when Thea looked desperately at her watch, it was still half-past eight. But her voice had dried to ash.

'I didn't get out of that pile-up.' Harry's smile was apologetic now. 'And, um – neither did you.'

Thea stared at the cut on Harry's forehead. And then at the deep gash on his neck. Self-consciously, Harry tightened his blue-green silk tie to cover it again, to steady his wobbling head.

'With me it was the plane, wasn't it? I

was a bit of a postscript, mind you.' Harry rolled his eyes fondly. 'I was on the same plane as Matt Cornwell. Remember?'

The mist was almost on them. The road disappeared into it just ahead, and there were still no other cars. But she remembered now. His plane. Her car. She remembered everything.

'I didn't see a diversion!'

'There's no diversion, Thea. No detours. Look.' Harry tapped his hand affectionately on Thea's white one, on the fingers locked in terror round the steering wheel. He nodded ahead.

'We're going now, Thea. Do watch the road in this mist.'

The Promise

by Mary Chapman

The Promise

by Mary Chapman

I peered at myself in the mirror.

'I'd do anything to get rid of these,' I muttered. 'One on my nose. Two on my chin. Three under my fringe – no, four! Another one's sprouted in the last minute!'

'You'd do *anything*?' said a voice behind me.

'Yes, anything!'

Without turning round I snapped, 'Jess,

get out of my room!'

Silence.

That wasn't like Jess. She'd always got something to say. Usually rude.

I turned round.

No Jess.

I opened the door. Nobody there.

Weird.

And what was even more weird, I thought I could smell smoke.

I rummaged around in the pile of stuff on my dressing-table.

ZAP! Zaps your Zits in seconds!

Well, that's what it said on the box. I bought it this morning. The girl at the chemists said it was good. But she gave me a pitying look. She didn't need it. She had beautiful, smooth skin, and didn't have to grow a fringe to hide behind.

I squeezed the cream out of the tube and

dabbed it on. One dab per spot. One. Two. Three. Four. Five. Six. Seven. Eight. Now there were nine! I'd soon be into double figures!

Saturday evening. My spots wouldn't have gone by Monday morning. I couldn't go to school looking like this.

The Zit plague started in the summer holidays. At the beginning of the holidays, my skin was like it had always been – clear and smooth. But when I went back in September, I was all spotty and pimply. Mum said it was part of growing up. Well, if it was, I didn't want to. I was *so* stressed. Everybody else in my year was growing up, but they weren't covered in zits. And that horrible Kim and her mate, Charlotte, started calling me Zitty Zoe. They said I'd got zits because I never washed my hair and ate too many sweets and chips. And that was *so* not true.

Sunday evening. The tube of *Zap!* was supposed to last five days, but I kept dabbing on another dollop of cream, and then another, until I'd used up the whole tube.

I'd smuggled a load of apples upstairs, and a huge bottle of mineral water. I thought – if I change my diet … So I'd had nothing all day, except apples and water.

I lay on my bed, eyes closed, feeling sick and empty. Tomorrow I'd persuade Mum I was too ill to go to school, but that wasn't the answer to the problem.

'I'd do anything to be rid of these zits,' I thought – well, I must have said it aloud, because I heard that voice again.

'*Anything*? You really mean that?'

'Yes!'

'Promise? If I get rid of them, you'll do *anything* I ask?'

The smell of smoke. Was the house on fire? I tried to open my eyes, but my eyelids felt so heavy I couldn't.

And another smell – sort of chemical, like the lab at school.

'You promise? You'll do *whatever* I ask?'

'Yeah, I promise, but who *are* you?'

'Never mind who I am. I'm here to help you,' said the voice. So soothing, friendly, caring. 'You're going to sleep now, Zoe, and when you wake in the morning your spots will have gone. Just don't forget your promise.'

But I was practically asleep.

When I woke in the morning, I had a fuzzy memory of a sort-of-dream. But I didn't give it any thought. I rushed over to the mirror, as usual, expecting to see the hated spots.

Not a single zit.

I lifted my fringe. My forehead was clear. My skin was glowing and radiant. That *Zap!* stuff really did work miracles. Maybe the water and apples had helped? I didn't need to hide away in my room any longer. I started to get ready for school.

I had a really good day. No nasty comments. I couldn't quite believe it. I kept having a quick peek in my little magnifying mirror. But it was true. No zits anywhere.

And that's how it went on. Every morning, I wondered if the zits had returned in the night. But, no, it was almost too good to be true. A miracle!

One Saturday night, a few days before Christmas, I was admiring myself in the mirror.

'Pleased with yourself, are you?' asked a voice.

'Go away, Jess!'

'No, not Jess,' said the voice. 'Your friend.'

'What friend?'

'The one who restored your beautiful complexion.'

'But that was the *Zap!* stuff,' I said. 'And apples and water.'

'No. It was me.'

Then I remembered my sort-of-dream. But the voice wasn't friendly this time. It was sharp. Less like honey. More like vinegar!

I'd better show I was grateful.

'Well, thank you very much,' I said. 'Everything's all right now. So I don't need any more help.'

'You haven't forgotten your promise, Zoe?'

'What promise?'

'That you'd do *anything* to be rid of your zits.'

Then I remembered.

'I just said that … like you do. It's just something people say.'

'Without meaning it?' The voice was cold, sharp as an icicle.

'Yes … I mean, no … '

'What *do* you mean, Zoe?'

'I didn't realise … I'm sorry. What do you want?'

'I want you to keep your promise. You made a pact with me. I don't take kindly to people who break promises.'

The voice was everywhere, behind me, over by the window, above me. It's not easy talking to an invisible being, darting about all over the room.

'Tell me what you want,' I said.

I could smell smoke, and that horrible chemical stink.

'I want your soul.'

'My … *what?*'

'Your soul. Spirit. Whatever you want to call it. Your mind. Brain. Personality. Consciousness. What makes you, Zoe, unique, different from everybody else, the only *you* in the world.'

'But – '

'You can keep your perfect complexion,' said the voice. 'I'm not bothered about that.'

'But what will happen to *me* if I give you my soul, or whatever it is?'

'You'll still look the same, but you'll be a bit … empty. Not sad. You won't feel anything. Nothing will hurt you. You won't be upset if people say horrible things to you.'

That would be good. Not to care what Kim and Charlotte said.

'Imagine that,' the voice continued. Gentle and friendly again.

'But if I don't feel anything … won't I feel happy?'

'What do you want to feel happy for? Happiness never lasts. It's over-rated, in my opinion. Better to feel nothing at all.'

I stared at my reflection.

What would it be like to feel absolutely nothing?

It would be great not to feel sad, frightened or jealous. But then I wouldn't feel happy, or confident, or loved. I'd be like a robot. I wouldn't dislike anything, but I wouldn't like anything either. I wouldn't feel enjoyment, or look forward to things, or feel relieved when nasty things, like exams, were over. I'd be a zombie. Life might be easier, but it would be very boring.

'Well?' said the voice. 'Time for the hand-over.'

'What do you mean?'

'You have to say you give me your soul freely.'

'I don't want to give it to you.'

'You promised. We made a pact.'

'I didn't realise – '

'I helped you. You owe me.'

'I'm very grateful.'

'Then keep your part of the bargain.' The voice was quiet now, menacing.

'I don't want to.' In the silence that followed, I felt my pulse thudding in my ears.

A swirl of smoke, bright flashes, that awful stench.

Sulphur!

'THEN TAKE YOUR PUNISHMENT!' the voice shrieked.

The room filled with smoke. I stumbled across to the window. Opened it wide. Breathed in the cold air.

Once the smoke cleared, I went back to my dressing-table. Looked in the mirror.

My face was scarlet and covered in zits.

I could see zits spreading down my neck. I felt them breaking out, all over my body. I ripped off my clothes. Every inch of my skin was bright red, tingling, itching, burning. I started scratching. I couldn't stop …

The doctor said it was an allergic reaction. But I knew different. I was terrified it would be like that for ever.

I had a rotten Christmas, but gradually the spots started to heal and fade. By Easter, they'd completely gone.

And then one evening, when I was getting ready for the school summer disco, I looked in the mirror and saw this huge zit on the end of my nose. More and more zits appeared, all over my face. They'd gone by the next morning, but I missed the disco.

In August, it was my cousin Melanie's wedding. I was chief bridesmaid. I was nervous. Would the zits return? But everything seemed to be OK. Until I went downstairs. Mum handed me my flowers and I had a last look in the hall mirror. The zits were back.

But I couldn't let Melanie down. Somehow, I got through the wedding.

Mum said it was stress. I don't think so.

After a few days, the zits disappeared – and they haven't come back … yet.

I don't know if I'll ever stop worrying about them.

One thing I do know. I'll never make another promise, unless I'm *absolutely sure* I can keep it.

The Hanging Tree

by Anne Rooney

The Hanging Tree

by Anne Rooney

Shadows lay like crooked fingers over the
path. They seemed to claw at the stones.
Alfie wondered if they were clawing their
way out or in. He looked up into the tree
that cast the shadows. It troubled him more
in winter than in summer. Those twig
fingers, poking at the sky, their ghosts
splayed on the path below. Alfie turned up

his collar and pulled his scarf tight around his neck, covering the lower part of his face. He felt his breath, damp and warm on the inside of the scarf.

'Why don't you like the tree?' Kayleigh asked, linking her arm through his.

'Do you think I don't like it?' he said.

Kayleigh laughed.

'It's obvious. You speed up to walk past it. And you sort of huddle up in your coat.'

It was true. Alfie hated the tree. He was sure on winter nights he had heard sounds coming from it. Rustling, even when there were no leaves. Or a low hissing that really couldn't be the wind.

'My grandfather told me about it,' he said.

'Tell me. I don't know any of the local tales,' Kayleigh said. 'I love that your family has always lived here. You know everything. Tell it to me as he told it to you.'

'It was more than two hundred years ago. Jack Tippett hid in a copse of trees on the hilltop. He'd done it many times before. It was cold. His horse snorted clouds of steamy breath that mixed with the fog. At last, a stagecoach rumbled up the hill. Jack pulled his scarf up over his face, so that just his eyes showed. He spurred his horse and galloped out in front of the coach. The coach horses reared up and whinnied in fright. Jack Tippett fired one of his three muskets in the air.

' "Stand and deliver!" he shouted.'

'He was a highwayman?' asked Kayleigh.

'Yes. The people stumbled from the stagecoach, trembling. They emptied their pockets and purses. But it went wrong. There was a boy in the stagecoach, called Benjamin Lucas. He clung to his mother's skirts and stared wide-eyed at the highwayman. He looked into Jack's green eyes above the scarf. He saw the curved scar that ran through his eyebrow.

' "Hello, Jack!" he called. And Jack fired his second musket into the boy's chest.'

Kayleigh shuddered.

'How horrible – he killed a little child?'

Alfie went on. 'Horrified at what he'd done, Jack turned his horse and galloped into the night. But next day, fourteen angry men were waiting for him. They beat him and bound him and dragged him to the tree – this tree. They tied a rope around his neck. Benjamin's uncle threw the end of the rope over a branch and hauled on it, dragging Jack Tippet up into the air. He struggled and kicked his legs. He went blue in the face; his tongue hung out. The men hit him with sticks and threw stones at him. Eventually, he stopped struggling.

But Jack Tippett didn't die in the tree. It began to rain. Hard rain, like iron rods, pelted the men and drove them back to seek cover. The hanging tree was blasted by lightning. It split down one side, dropping Jack Tippett to the ground. He ran through the grey spears of rain, the noose around his neck and the rope trailing in the mud.'

'What happened to him?'

'No one knows. He ran and ran. People say he runs still. He can never find rest. Not unless he finds someone to take his place in the hanging tree. Someone must pay for the hurt done to Benjamin Lucas.'

Kayleigh shivered. 'But it's just a story,' she said.

'It's a true story.'

'What, even about him still wandering the Earth? Do you believe that?'

'No,' said Alfie. But he wasn't sure.

They were right by the tree. Kayleigh pointed ahead, just to the left of the path.

'Look! Alfie, look at that bird! What's it doing?'

Alfie peered into the fog. 'It's just a magpie.'

'One for sorrow,' said Kayleigh. 'What's it doing? Look, it's got something in its beak.'

Alfie looked again. Something gold glittered in the bird's beak. There was a red stone, too, sparkling.

'It's got a gold and ruby ring!' he said.

At his voice, the magpie flapped its wings and rose into the fog. But it didn't go far. It landed on a branch, just above them. It took three steps sideways along the branch, then dipped its head. When it flew down again, its beak was empty.

'It must have put it in its nest,' said Kayleigh. 'Climb up and get it. Please.'

Alfie swallowed. He didn't want to refuse. He didn't want her to think he was scared.

'It's nearly dark,' he said. 'I won't be able to see properly. Look at the fog.'

'You'll be able to see gold,' she said. 'It will sparkle. Go on. Please. I'd love a gold ring.'

Alfie held out his arms.

'Look,' he said, 'I'm in my school clothes. They're not good for tree climbing.'

Kayleigh laughed.

'They'll be fine. Are you scared?'

'No!' he said. 'But ... No, of course not. I just don't think I'll be able to climb in these.'

Kayleigh touched his cheek. Her fingers were soft and cool.

'Please get it for me.'

Alfie dropped his school bag on the ground, but he still didn't move. They stood looking at each other. Then Kayleigh threw down her own bag on top of his.

'Fine,' she said. 'I'll get it myself. I'm not scared of a stupid magpie. Or a tree.'

'I'm not scared,' Alfie protested. But it was too late. She was already pulling herself up, fingers twined around the thick stems of ivy that strangled the trunk. He stood watching, not sure what to do.

'Careful,' he called.

She looked over her shoulder at him. It was a disdainful look that made him embarrassed. She carried on climbing.

A flurry of ivy leaves fell to the ground in front of Alfie. At the same time, Kayleigh cried out.

'What is it?' he asked, peering upwards.

Kayleigh whimpered, stifling a sob. Her left foot was at an awkward angle, her right foot scrabbling for a foothold a little above his head, her fingers gripping the ivy.

'Are you OK?' he asked.

'No. I've hurt my ankle. My foot's stuck and I twisted it. Owwww,' she whimpered again. Alfie thought she would cry.

'Do you want me to help you?' he asked.

'Yes, please. Help me down and then get the ring.'

'What? You still want it?' He was angry now. It was a stupid thing to do, climb the hanging tree in the dark and the fog, just for a ring. Couldn't she see now that it was stupid?

'I was just unlucky. You're good at climbing – you'll be fine.'

'Hang on. I'll get you down, at least.' He had no intention of getting the ring, though.

He dug his fingers into cracks in the bark between the ivy and pulled himself up. The bark was wet and slippery with fog. But the tree wasn't hard to climb. Six feet above the ground it forked and after that branches came thick and fast.

Kayleigh was just past the fork. He soon reached her. He guided her right foot onto a solid branch, then gently lifted her left foot out of her shoe. She cried out as he twisted it, but then it was free and he showed her where to put it. He tossed the shoe to the ground and waited while she climbed down, guiding her to handholds as she passed him.

'Thank you,' she said, as her feet touched the ground. 'Can you see the nest?'

'Are you mad? Hasn't it been enough trouble already?'

'Go on Alfie, please! You aren't scared, are you? You're almost there now.'

What could he do? If he refused, she'd tell everyone he was scared. She wouldn't like him any more. It would only take a minute.

The place the bird had landed was to his left. It was in a bare part of the tree that forked and jutted out over the space below. Alfie pulled himself up to the branch and inched along it. He could see an untidy, dark shape through the gloom. It must be the nest. Twigs from above caught in his hair and snagged his clothes. They scratched his face and snatched at his hood. He shuffled along the branch, carefully, slowly.

'Hsssss.'

Alfie's neck prickled. He looked down at Kayleigh. She was beneath, looking up at him. Silent. What sound do magpies make?

'Hsssss.' There it was again – like a hiss or a whisper. Was he imagining it? He tried to look around, to see if there was someone else there.

But the magpie was back. It flew at his face making him jump. He lurched backwards and had to grab at the branch so that he didn't fall. The bird flapped its wings at him and made a loud, chattering sound, trying to drive him away.

Alfie tried to shuffle back along the branch, but he felt something cold and sharp poke at his neck. He twisted his head quickly, but it only jabbed him harder. He couldn't turn his head back. Whatever had caught him was under his scarf. Rising panic made him wriggle. That made it worse. He raised a hand to his neck, but couldn't reach behind him. And the magpie flew at him again, straight at his face. He thrashed at it, but lost his balance. He snatched at the branch. His hand touched something hard and cold – something that moved away under his hand. He pulled his hand away again.

'Hsssss.'

Alfie teetered on the branch. The magpie flew at his face again, and he swiped wildly at it.

'Be careful!' shouted Kayleigh.

He twisted round at her voice, and the scarf tightened. His leg slid over the branch and into empty space. He grabbed at the branch, but his hand closed on nothing as he fell …

Then he jerked to a halt. All his muscles jolted. He couldn't breathe. The scarf pulled tight around his neck. He reached up but he couldn't loosen it – his body weight pulled it tight. He kicked and struggled, his feet flailing around in the air seeking a branch. But there were no branches, just open, empty air and the ground far below. He saw Kayleigh's mouth open to scream.

The pain in Alfie's neck and chest was unbearable. He gasped desperately for breath, but none came.

Suddenly, something gripped Alfie's

wrist. Something icy and sharp, and brittle as twigs.

The surrounding darkness closed in on him and he stopped struggling.

'*Shhhhh.*'

It seemed that the fog itself whispered to him.

Another hand grabbed his shoulder. The fingers were as thin as knife blades. They dug deep into Alfie's flesh. He felt like meat hung on a meat hook. Dead meat. That's what he was. But then he was rising through the air. Yes, surely he was rising? The meat hooks were lifting him up into the tree. The pressure on his neck became less.

One hand released him, the other digging further into his flesh as it took his weight.

Alfie tried to protest, but he had no breath. Then, in front of his face, he saw

half a grey-white face with spaces where
the eyes should be and black hair hanging
in tatters over and around it. The bottom
half of the face was hidden. Was it behind
a scarf? Or was it eaten away by the fog, or
worse? Alfie couldn't tell. He felt something
cold at his neck, something besides the wet
scarf. Metal. A blade. He tried again to
kick and flailed his legs. He struggled to get
his free hand to his throat.

'Hsssss.'

That sound again, but right beside his
ear this time.

The blade nicked his neck. It was icy
cold, colder than ice. The coldest thing he
had ever felt. The tightness at his neck
eased a little, and then a little more. And
then it was gone. Two halves of the scarf
fell to the ground and then something else,
something that made a dull sound as it hit

the leaves. The meat hooks were back in his flesh, in both his wrists now. Alfie gulped in huge gasps of air, filling his empty lungs. His head was swimming, he felt faint. All he could see was the half-face, its empty eye sockets windows on to the darkness behind.

'Hsssss.'

Alfie whimpered.

'Who – what are you?' he managed to say.

'Hsssssss,' it whispered. And then, very quietly, '*Jack*.'

The meat-hook fingers lowered Alfie, and then they were gone. He fell to the ground. The wet leaves were thick and cold beneath him. At once, the magpie rose into the air, and Kayleigh was beside him.

'Are you all right? What happened? I was so scared. I thought you'd be strangled!'

Alfie didn't answer. The tree loomed above him, a sprawling, black shape against the fog. A patch of thicker fog seemed to hang in the tree. He thought he heard a sound again, '*Hsssss.*' But he couldn't be sure.

He saw, above him, the magpie with the ring in its beak once again. It stood on a branch and looked at him, cocking its head to one side.

Alfie put his hand out to push himself up. It met something thin, and colder than the leaves. His fingers closed on the blade and he picked it up. A folding knife.

'What happened?' Kayleigh said again.

'Jack,' Alfie said. 'He's paid his debt.' He held out his hand, the knife lying in his palm. The bone handle was worn and scratched, but he could just make out the initials carved into it: J.T.

The Land Rover

by John Townsend

The Land Rover

by John Townsend

The track was a jungle of nettles and brambles.

'Even Tarzan wouldn't get past this lot!' Tom sat on a tree stump and took a swig from his can.

Ali was keen to go home. 'Let's forget it. There won't be anything there.'

Tom stood on the stump. 'I can see

something. It's a roof. It must be one of the sheds. I've got to take a look while we're here.'

Ali sighed. 'It'll take all day. Why don't we come back at the weekend with hedge cutters?'

'Hey – that's one of your best ideas yet.'

Tom had never met his great, great Uncle Edgar. The old man had locked himself away for years in the farmhouse. He never let anyone come to see him. And that's where he died, two months ago, at the grand age of ninety-nine. The police had to break down his front door. He'd been dead for days.

Ali went with Tom to the funeral, where they were surprised at how many people turned up. Uncle Edgar had been quite famous and had won medals in the Second World War. Then he'd worked in Africa, before hiding away in his old farmhouse, which became a real tip and full of junk. It took weeks to clear everything out, before anyone could start on the sheds and barns.

For most of Saturday, Tom and Ali hacked their way up the track to a row of sheds. The timber was rotten. Ivy and brambles had taken hold.

'No one's been here for fifty years, I reckon,' Tom said. 'This shed's like Fort Knox. Look at those chains and locks!'

They needed bolt-cutters to open the door, even though its hinges had almost rusted through. A curtain of cobwebs shimmered where bats hung from the rafters. Rats scuttled, as light spilled inside. The first light for fifty years.

'Yuk. What a smell of mould. I'm not going in there!' Ali stood outside while Tom went in.

'Help me pull the other door open,' he

called. 'I need more light. There's something in here.'

Shafts of dusty light cut through the gloom, where a rotten rug covered something big.

'I don't like it,' Ali said. 'There's something scary here. I felt an icy shiver. I tell you, Tom – I don't like it.'

But Tom was already pulling the rug to the floor, in a cloud of dust. Ali sneezed and turned away. Old, rat-chewed sacks slid to the ground as Tom stood back, his mouth wide open. 'Wow! Just look at that beauty!'

Ali shrugged. 'Big deal,' she said. But Tom was already wiping the bonnet. 'Don't you see, Ali? It's an old Series One Land Rover. I'd kill to get my hands on one of these!'

They didn't hear the sound. Like something stirring.

It took a week to clear the track for the pick-up truck to tow away the Land Rover. Tom's dad said he could keep the old Land Rover to work on. Even though it was in a bad way, for Tom it was like a dream come true. The tyres were no good and a lot of the bodywork had rusted. The front seats were eaten by rats and the engine needed major work. But Tom was keen to give it a go. He and some work mates spent all their spare time repairing and re-building it.

'My Series One Land Rover was made between 1948 and 1953,' Tom told everyone. 'It's an 80-inch wheelbase and I'm fitting a 1595cc petrol engine.'

He went on about the gears, front wheel drive and every new rivet and screw.

It took over his life. Ali hardly saw him and had to phone to ask how he was getting on.

'Don't worry,' he said. 'You'll soon be joining me on my first drive in it.'

'You must be joking,' she snapped. 'That Land Rover gives me the creeps. You'll never get me inside that thing.'

Late at night, while working alone, Tom removed the back seat. He wasn't ready for what he found hidden under it. He lifted out a small leather case. But that wasn't all. He stood back in horror. Beside it, wrapped in cloth, was a human skull.

'I knew there was something weird about that thing,' Ali said. 'I feel cold inside if I go anywhere near it.'

'Really?' Tom said. 'It's not so with me. Sometimes when I'm working inside it I get really hot.'

Ali began going through letters and photos in the old case.

'It seems your Uncle Edgar took the Land

Rover to Egypt in 1949. He went with his wife, your Auntie May, to explore old tombs. Here's a photo of the Land Rover by a pyramid. And there's Uncle Edgar with his arm round a young woman. She must be Auntie May.'

Tom looked at the photo. 'She looks really cool.'

Ali flicked his ear. 'Auntie May, or your precious Land Rover?'

'The Land Rover, of course!'

'Tom! Poor Auntie May died just after that photo. There's a letter here. Listen to this.

'*My poor May died in her tent last night. It was so sudden. They say it was a snake bite. I'm not so sure. It could be the curse of the tomb. The skull was beside her in the tent.*'

A cold wind blew as Tom went back to the workshop. He looked at the skull on a pile

58

of oily rags. Could there really be a curse?

The heat hit him as soon as he opened the Land Rover. A dry, intense heat and a strange smell. The driver's seat was covered in fine sand. He was sure he heard the buzzing of flies … followed by something else. The hiss of a snake.

Tom ran into the house. He didn't tell Ali about the noises in the Land Rover. But he needed to know more. They found a note that Uncle Edgar wrote, after he came home from Egypt.

'The curse has followed me home. This morning Patsy was playing in the bedroom. I saw her touch the skull on the shelf. It was the last time I saw her alive. Dear Patsy was just six. Doctors said her arm was swollen from deadly poison – from a scorpion sting.

It's time to do something fast. I should never have dug up that skull. It should be left to rest in peace. I will hide every memory of that fateful Egypt trip. I can't bear to see the Land Rover any more. It must all be hidden forever.'

'There's only one thing for it,' Tom said. 'I'll have to put that skull to rest. I'll nail it in a wooden box and bury it at the bottom of the garden.'

He dug a deep hole under the holly tree and buried the box inside. After filling the hole with soil and stamping turf on top, he went back to the workshop and sat in the Land Rover. He waited. Nothing. There were no sounds. It was cool and still.

'I've cracked it!' he smiled. 'Another few weeks and this will be on the road.'

Ali put all the papers back in the case and stood at the window. She thought about poor Auntie May and Patsy … until she saw what was down the garden. The holly tree's leaves were brown and falling.

They blew across the dead grass. Nothing grew at the bottom of the garden. There was a bare patch where Tom had buried the box. No birds would go near.

The Land Rover was looking good. Tom and his mates had done a great job. The engine and the bodywork were as good as new when the day came to go on the road for the first time. People came to watch the big launch. The local paper printed the story: *HIDDEN FOR HALF A CENTURY*. It told of Tom's hard work and printed the photo of Uncle Edgar by a pyramid.

The Land Rover was great to drive. It handled well in ice and snow. But then Tom heard the buzzing of flies again. The heat inside became so unbearable he had to get out in the freezing wind to cool down. He didn't tell anyone – even when he became ill.

The doctors said Tom must have caught malaria when he'd been abroad. He had to rest, so he left the Land Rover in the garage for months – until an American phoned.

'Hi, Tom. We've seen all the stuff about your old Land Rover. Can we use it? We're making a movie. Of course, we'll pay you.'

Tom felt really proud when the film crew came to drive the Land Rover away, but he wasn't prepared for the call a few days later – nor the headline in the paper.

FILM STAR KILLED BY COBRA.

She died on the film set … while sitting in Tom's Land Rover.

With the Land Rover back in his garage, Tom decided to get rid of it.

'It's for the best. It upsets me, but who knows what may happen next?'

He paused as he held Ali's hand. 'I can't

drive it any more. There's something about it. Uncle Edgar knew that. I'll have to destroy it. Tonight when it's dark, I'm going to dump it in the lake.'

They looked down into the murky water of Tarn Lake. Tom felt sick – not just from what he was about to do, but from driving the Land Rover. Even with all the windows open, the heat and smell inside had been too much. Ali had driven her Mini – to take them home again.

Tom released the hand brake and stood back. The Land Rover rolled forward. He couldn't watch as his pride and joy plunged down the bank. It hit the water and spun onto its roof. A sheet of spray shot across the lake. Within seconds, the wheels sank below the bubbling water. Down and down. Down to the dark and muddy depths.

Ali held Tom's hand and led him away.

He was unable to speak as they drove back in the darkness.

No one mentioned the Land Rover for days … until they saw the News on TV. A reporter was standing on the bank of Tarn Lake. She told the chilling news of an angler found floating in the icy water. But he hadn't drowned. He'd died from a snake bite to his neck.

Ali rushed outside. She needed to think. She looked down the garden, to the skull's resting place. At least the grass was growing again now. The holly tree was green once more. That was some relief. Except …

Her heart missed a beat. For there, under the holly tree, lay the skull … gleaming in the moonlight … staring up at her.

Grinning.